SILENT NIGHT

THE SONG FROM HEAVEN

Linda Granfield

Art by Nelly and Ernst Hofer

Tundra Books

The author and illustrators would like to express their gratitude to the Tundra and McClelland & Stewart staff for their insights, expertise, and patience. They would also like to thank the Metropolitan Toronto Reference Library; Gabriele Neureiter of the Keltenmuseum, Hallein, Austria; Rita Vost in Switzerland; the Stratford Public Library; the Listowel Public Library; and their supportive families who kept their wits when "all" was *not* calm.

Published in Canada by Tundra Books, *McClelland & Stewart Young Readers*,
481 University Avenue, Toronto, Ontario M5G 2E9

Published in the United States by Tundra Books of Northern New York,
P.O. Box 1030, Plattsburgh, New York 12901

Library of Congress Catalog Number: 97-60484

Canadian Cataloguing in Publication Data

Granfield, Linda
    Silent night : the song from heaven

ISBN 0-88776-395-2

1. Gruber, Franz Xaver, 1787-1863. Stille Nacht, heilige Nacht. 2. Mohr, Joseph, 1792-1848. Stille Nacht, heilige Nacht. I. Hofer, Nelly. II. Hofer, Ernst, 1961- . III. Title.

ML410.G931G75 1997   j782.28'1723   C97-930628-0

We acknowledge the support of the Canada Council for the Arts for our publishing program.

Book design: Brian Bean

Printed and bound in Canada

1 2 3 4 5 6   02 01 00 99 98 97

In loving memory of my father, Joseph J. Granfield.
Sleep in heavenly peace.
L. G.

For our parents, Bertha and Otto Graber and Marie and Ernst Hofer,
who have offered a lifetime of love and support.
N. H. and E. H.

1818

Oberndorf, Austria

HANS AND MARIA, coated and capped, hurry through the icy cobbled streets to the Church of St. Nicola. It is the day before Christmas, and all the villagers are preparing for the holiday. Travelers swaddled in heavy woolen clothing shout happy greetings to one another as they drive their sleighs over the snowy roads. The air is tangy with the rich aromas of baked pies and fresh fish for Christmas Eve. Best of all, it is time to build the Christmas crèche.

INSIDE THE CHURCH, the preparations have begun. Rough bark and moss cover the manger walls; dry rushes form a sloped roof, and mottled stone curves into the ancient walls of Bethlehem. Each wax figure is lifted from its box. Under the watchful eyes of their parents, children carefully dust the thick folds of the carved garments, and select the perfect place for each figure. Wise Joseph and Mary, veiled in blue, soon gaze lovingly upon their newborn Son, lying in the straw-filled manger.

"Was it cold on that night long ago?" whispered Maria. "Did the Baby see His breath in the frosty air, like I do?"

THE CHILDREN BRING the waxen lambs, white and gray. And the shepherds, with carved burrs in their beards and tattered robes that brush their travel-worn sandals, are placed around the sleeping Babe. Leaning on their crooks, the shepherds ignore their sheep and strain to see the Child's face.

"Did the lambs keep the Baby warm on that night long ago?" whispered Hans. "Did their bleating chase sleep away from the Little One?"

TALL CAMELS, LONG-LASHED and heavy-lidded, stand stiffly on the children's sleds in procession to the crèche. The tiny silver bells sewn on their blankets tinkle as the children arrange the camels in the shade of carved palm trees.

And beside these mute beasts are placed the Three Wise Men, dressed in crimson and sapphire silken finery. Brushes, dipped in gold and silver paints, repair their crowns and fill the cracks in their polished urns and burnished chests.

"Did the Little One hear the music of camel bells on that night long ago?" whispered Maria. "Did He smell the sweet incense and perfumes?"

THEN COME THE angels, their feather-heavy waxen wings arranged to watch over St. Nicola's crèche. Angelic mouths open wide to silently proclaim the birth of the Child. Gleaming banners echo the angels' joyous song. High on the roof of the manger, heaven's messengers beckon everyone to come closer.

"Did a feather from an angel's wing tickle the Baby on that night long ago?" whispered Hans. "Did the angels' voices crack like Uncle Otto's?"

AT LAST! THE solemn figures are in place. Maria moves the lambs closer to the Baby's crib, "to keep Him warm," she says. Hans helps Uncle Otto move the heavy ladder, for it is time to hang the star. Aunt Bertha smooths the tinseled comet. The smell of fresh pine boughs fills the air.

In Hans's fingers, the star rises to the heavens. Its golden tail streams behind it and rests to touch the painted clouds hanging high above the angels. The storage boxes, now filled only with straw, are put away. The floor is soon swept clean.

"Could the Baby sleep in the star's amber glow on that night long ago?" whispered Maria. "Did He fuss and awaken?"

THE LONG AFTERNOON'S work is done, and evening fills the Church of St. Nicola. The wooden fence has been wrapped around the crèche, and the children light candles. Hans can hear every footstep on the cold, stone floor; all the noise of the day seems to have been packed away with the empty boxes.

Father Mohr brushes the snow from his shoulders as he enters the church. He grumbles to Uncle Otto that the organ isn't working, that midnight mass will be different this year. But in the quiet, everyone silently gazes at the splendid scene. In the flickering candlelight, the wax figures glow with life. And once again, as on every Christmas Eve for as long as Maria can remember, the villagers of Oberndorf share the story of that blessed night in Bethlehem.

"Did the Holy Child hear a sweet lullaby on that night so long ago?" whispered Hans. "I'd sing one for Him," said Maria.

Father Josef Mohr was born in 1792. He sang sacred music as a boy, became a priest, and was appointed to the Church of St. Nicola in Oberndorf, Austria.

Franz Xaver Gruber, born in 1787, studied to become a teacher and, in 1807, became the schoolmaster and organist in Arnsdorf, a village near Oberndorf. Father Mohr and Gruber became friends when the teacher traveled to play the organ at St. Nicola.

On the day before Christmas, 1818, the church organ was broken. Perhaps the constant damp from the nearby Salzach River had rusted parts of the instrument.

A more entertaining explanation involves hungry mice. Driven inside by the fierce winter cold, the tiny animals found the organ's leather bellows very tasty. Consequently, the mice chewed a hole that crippled the instrument.

Since unaccompanied singing was unpopular in those days, Father Mohr asked Gruber to compose music for the verses he'd written that day. Within a few hours, Gruber matched notes to the words of the new song for voice and guitar that eventually became known as "Silent Night."

After the holiday, Karl Mauracher was called to repair the organ. It is believed that he took the new song home with him and shared it with musicians and singers he met. "Stille Nacht," however, became a forgotten title. The song was called "The Song From Heaven" and was said to be of "unknown origin."

During the mid-1800s, groups of strolling, family singers

performed in the streets and often gave concerts. The talented Strasser family were such a group of entertainers. The four Strasser children performed "The Song From Heaven" whenever their glove-maker parents traveled to fairs to sell their goods. By 1832, the Strassers had taken the song to Leipzig and introduced it to German audiences.

In 1839, another singing family, the Rainers, took the song to the United States and performed it for delighted audiences. "The Song From Heaven" was soon included in prayer books and hymnals.

As the song's popularity grew, Father Mohr and Gruber were all but forgotten. Some people believed "The Song From Heaven" had been written by Mozart, Beethoven, or Franz Joseph Haydn's brother, Johann Michael. Others thought it was a Tyrolean folk song.

In 1854, musical authorities in Berlin sent to Salzburg and asked if the Haydn manuscript was in St. Peter's Church. As it happened, Felix Gruber, Franz's youngest son, was a choirboy at the church. He told his father about the request.

Gruber had left St. Nicola in 1829 and was living near Salzburg in Hallein. He attempted to settle the debate by writing a document entitled "The Authentic Occasion for the Writing of the Christmas Song 'Silent Night, Holy Night.'"

Thirty-six years after "Stille Nacht" was first performed in a cold village church, its worldwide audience finally learned the identities of its humble and gifted creators.

Father Mohr left St. Nicola in 1819. He died and was buried in Wagrain in December, 1848. His friend Gruber lived until 1863.

One of the most moving stories about the song took place during the horrors of World War I. On Christmas Eve, 1914, in the dark European trenches, the freezing men awaited the next attack by the enemy soldiers across no man's land. But there was no shooting. Only silence. Afraid to peer over the top of the trench, the British soldiers quietly sat and listened to the rising sound of men's voices singing.

When they dared to look across the battle-scarred terrain, the British saw the gleam of tiny lights, as the Germans lit candles on small Christmas trees in their trenches. "Stille Nacht" filled the air as the German soldiers observed the holy eve of peace.

In a desolate landscape far from home, the soldiers of both sides called a truce. They embraced, shared cigars, chocolate and sausages. On Christmas Day, they played soccer on the battlefield.

The unofficial truce lasted for days but, eventually, the men returned to the business at hand – war – for nearly four more years.

After World War I, the popularity of "Silent Night" continued to grow. In the 1920s and 30s, radio listeners heard the song performed by many singers, including Franz Gruber's own grandson who played it on Father Mohr's guitar.

Famous contralto, Madame Ernestine Schumann-Heink, sang "Stille Nacht" each Christmas Eve on the radio in what became a holiday tradition for families around the world. "Mother" Schumann-Heink also recorded it for play on phonographs. Translations enabled people everywhere to share the song.

The deteriorating original Church of St. Nicola was torn down around 1900. The small Stille Nacht Kapelle (Silent Night Chapel) was built in Oberndorf to commemorate Father Josef Mohr and Franz Xaver Gruber and, every Christmas Eve, a special service is held outside the chapel.

Whether it is heard in a snow-covered Alpine village or under a blazing African sky, "Silent Night" invites us to reflect on the meaning of Christmas and to "sleep in heavenly peace."

Scherenschnitt

I n 1818, when "Silent Night" was first written, many families' homes were decorated with beautiful art created from nothing but paper. *Scherenschnitt* – the German word for silhouette – is an art believed to have originated in Asia centuries ago. Wondrously detailed pictures were created in China by cutting a single piece of parchment, turning the knife to make the smallest cut, creating an entire scene without glue.

By the end of the seventeenth century, travelers to Asia had brought the technique to Europe. Less expensive paper replaced the parchment, and designs were still cut with knives. In 1759, the French finance minister, Etienne de Silhouette, known for his thriftiness, recommended cut-paper portraits as economical alternatives to costly oil paintings. People began to cut and collect "silhouettes," the snapshots of the day.

Silhouette artists traveled the countryside and for a fee, cut with great speed and accuracy, the portraits of people they met. In Germany, Switzerland, Austria, and North America, black-and-white papers were popular. In Eastern Europe and Asia, colored papers were selected most often.

The advent of photography in the mid-1800s gave the public an alternate way to capture their likenesses, but the art of *scherenschnitt* survived. Today's artists cut the designs with extremely sharp, tiny-bladed scissors – and steady hands. The *scherenschnitte* in this book are evidence of a special gift passed from generation to generation, to tease and delight the eye of the beholder.

Silent night, holy night,	Stille Nacht, heilige Nacht
All is calm, all is bright.	Alles schläft, einsam wacht
Round yon Virgin Mother and Child,	Nur das traute hoch heilige Paar.
Holy Infant so tender and mild,	Holder Knabe mit lokkigem Haar.
Sleep in heavenly peace;	Schlaf in himmlischer Ruh,
Sleep in heavenly peace.	Schlaf in himmlischer Ruh.
Silent night, holy night,	Stille Nacht, heilige Nacht
Shepherds quake at the sight.	Hirten erst kund gemacht;
Glories stream from heaven afar,	Durch der Engel Halleluja
Heav'nly hosts sing Alleluia;	Tönt es laut von fern und nah:
Christ the Savior is born;	Christ, der Retter, ist da.
Christ the Savior is born.	Christ, der Retter, ist da.